A catalogue record for this book is available
from the British Library

Published by Ladybird Books Ltd
27 Wrights Lane London W8 5TZ
A Penguin Company
3 5 7 9 10 8 6 4

Printed in Italy

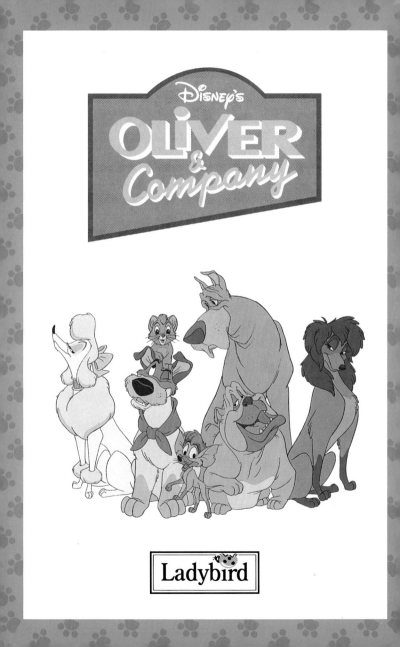

One by one, the kittens had been sold. Now only Oliver was left. He sat on the New York City pavement, very lonely. Suddenly he smelled something wonderful. The hot-dog man was cooking sausages!

As Oliver moved hopefully towards him, someone said, "Let's team up. You jump on him – I'll grab the sausages." It was Dodger, leader of Fagin's gang of pocket-picking dogs.

Oliver wasn't keen on dogs, but he *was* hungry. He jumped on the hot-dog man's shoe. Next moment, he saw Dodger disappearing, complete with sausages.

Moving fast, Dodger made for the old barge in Manhattan where Fagin and his gang lived. Oliver was close on his heels, hungrier than ever.

The gang began to plan. "Let's fix a pretend car accident," said Tito. "Then we can go through the back pockets of the crowd."

Oliver found the next few minutes confusing. The gang went into action, car brakes squealed, and somehow he finished up *inside* the car.

There was a little girl called Jenny in the car. The driver, Winston, was looking after her while her parents were away. She cuddled Oliver and said, "Oh Winston, the poor thing's half starved!"

Oliver purred. He had wanted a special person of his own — and here she was!

"Don't worry," said Dodger.
"We'll get her back. Absitively."

They all crowded onto Fagin's
scooter – even Georgette – and
hurried across town to Sykes'
warehouse.

There they found Jenny, tied up
in a chair.

Two huge Dobermans guarded the warehouse, but the gang went smoothly into action. Some drew off the watchdogs while the others broke in and freed Jenny.

"Hurry!" cried Fagin, and they all piled back on his scooter to make their getaway.

Oliver watched in horror as Sykes bundled Jenny into the car.

"You can't do that," yelled Fagin.

Sykes grinned wickedly. "You've done me a good turn. You don't owe me anything now," he shouted back, then drove off rapidly.

Oliver was very upset. He thought Jenny had gone for ever.

When Jenny read the note, she said miserably, "It says if I don't pay them, I will never see Oliver again. Come on, Georgette, we'll take my piggy bank. Perhaps that will be enough to get him back."

As they set out, Georgette sighed. She was just going to have to put up with Oliver for Jenny's sake.

The moment Fagin saw Jenny, he knew he had made a mistake. But before he could give Oliver back, Sykes drove up.

"This one's worth more than a cat!" he said, grabbing Jenny.

"That family must be rich. They'll pay to get him back and we can pay Sykes. If I tell him what's happening, he'll give us more time."

He began to write a ransom note.

Dear Mr Very Rich Cat Owner Person,

Alas, Sykes had seen them. He set off in hot pursuit. Even when they rode down the steps to the railway, he was close behind.

Then just as they reached the railway line, his car rammed the overloaded scooter. Jenny went flying through the air.

She landed on the bonnet of Sykes' car. Oliver and Dodger leapt to help her but Dodger fell through the sun roof onto the Dobermans.

Then everyone panicked as a train came thundering towards them. Fagin turned to grab Jenny, and Tito steered the scooter off the track.

Seconds later, the train hit the car, sending it hurtling into the river below.

With it went Dodger and Oliver.

Long unhappy minutes passed as Jenny, Georgette and the gang stared down into the water.

No one spoke.

Suddenly Dodger appeared, carrying a limp Oliver. Still no one spoke. Then, as Jenny gently took him in her arms, Oliver gave a faint miaow. And they all began to talk at once.

He was alive.

Next day Jenny gave a grand birthday party with what Dodger called "An absitively gynormous birthday cake."

The gang sang Happy Birthday cheerfully – and Georgette smiled at Oliver.